Remember,
My Child

Jade Anschultz

Fulton Books, Inc.
Meadville, PA

Published by Fulton Books 2021

ISBN 978-1-63710-891-8 (paperback)
ISBN 978-1-63710-893-2 (hardcover)
ISBN 978-1-63710-892-5 (digital)

Printed in the United States of America

Daughter, may your glass always be full. If by chance it runs dry, remember your filling stations so that you may refuel, and then continue on your dreams and adventures. I love you, Sadie Fay.

Stay kind, my child. Even when someone doesn't play fair.

Stay strong, my child. Even
when the world seems
too tough to bear.

Stay humble, my child. Even when you feel like one billion bucks.

Persevere, my child. Even when you
think that you've run out of luck.

Stay brave, my child. Even when you feel a little bit scared.

Be giving, my child. Even when you think that you don't really want to share.

Always set goals, my child. And never, ever settle.

Get dirty, my child. Never be too proud for that.

Sing and dance, my child. Even if your tune comes out a little flat.

Be observant, my child. Always appreciate the creation around.

Keep your head up, my child. Know if
you're lost, you can always be found.

Be confident, my child. Know that
home can always be your place.

16

Know that I love you, my child. Even when
I'm not there to say it to your face.

About the Author

Meet the author, Jade Anschultz of Arkansas. She is a NICU nurse, hairstylist, eyelash extension artist, guitar player, singer, wife, and mother to one young daughter. Her writing endeavors began when she was young, but her passions shifted with motherhood by wanting to teach life lessons in ways that her book-loving daughter would enjoy. Jade has a passion for summarizing morals that are important to her and writing them out for children to understand. She creates these fun stories to list values that she wants her daughter, and all who read her books, to carry with them not only as a young child soaking in a book, but also into growing years and beyond. She has chosen to release these stories to the world so that it may allow families of all kinds to open the door in discussing the message behind the story.

CPSIA information can be obtained
at www.ICGtesting.com
Printed in the USA
LVHW071045200422
716610LV00007B/174